KRYPTOS

KRYPTOS

(Jason Balan)

by

Tom Allsworth

Dedication

To

To Jan my eternal wife, my companion, my lover, my
sweetheart.
Without her support, I could never put pen to paper.

To Rachel, our Kissy daughter, who keeps a smile on our
faces.

To Arthur (age 7) who helped me see the joy of playing
with toy soldiers again.

With thanks to Royal Marine C/Sgt
Wayne Sanderson
For advice on jungle survival and munitions

CONTENTS

CHAPTER 1

Jason Balan waited for his boss to arrive and read a book under his breath to pass the time. His boss, Aaron Ford, sat down at his desk as he entered the room.

The well-thumbed book was closed after the dog-eared page. He declared he liked jaguars. "I have total respect for how they catch and dispatch their quarry."

"How many times have you read that book?

"I lost count," said Jason Balan. "They can teach us a lot in our trade."

Ford threw a folder across the desk.

After turning it, he read the title on the cover. Jason started reading the first page after opening it.

"A Utah man with a possible Yucatec Maya ancestry was born to a second generation of immigrants from Colombia."

"Four years at the University resulted in an honors degree."

"He could lead a lacrosse team to success."

"With several successful operations to his credit, Balan is well-seasoned and has gained a firearm qualification with ease."

"His six-foot-three frame and firm body belie his inner charm and ability to spot ways to lift others with personal frailties."

"Assigned to lead a new Rapid Response Team."

At the news, his expression did not show the increase in his heartbeat.

"The power players above us have enlarged the number of teams. They have decided that you will be the leader of the Rapid Response Team."

He was about to turn the page but stopped as Ford's hand hit the folder.

"Ford reminded him of the strict nature of non-disclosure of appointment or service before he read any further. Do you agree and understand?"

Without thought, Jason responded, "Yes."

"Read on, said Ford.

Jason read the known history of a man branded 'El Fantasma,' a Colombian drug baron, so called because of his ability to vanish.

There was a knock on the door. Ford invited the person to enter. A young lady with flowing blonde hair stood in the doorway.

"Pretty," mused Jason.

Ford invited her to enter.

"Jason, meet Cora Vale, your intelligence specialist."

Jason rose to shake her hand, but she moved towards the large flat screen on the opposite wall. There was a high-resolution satellite image of a dense rain forest on the screen.

"This is the best image we have of where we suspect El Fantasma receives cocaine from," said Cora. "The coca farm is on a bend of the Rio Caquetá, 500 miles south of Bogota, Colombia."

He was interested in what she had to say, but his interests included her very shapely form, her long slender legs that disappeared beneath the hem of her dress, and her perfect 'photoshopped' face.

The girls he had known were beautiful, but he had never seen such beauty.

His mind raced as he looked at her figure.

"Mr. Balan, I trust you are taking this all in. We fly to Bogota Monday morning."

Ford sniggered at Jason's embarrassment.

Ford said. "The code name of the operation is Eek."

Jason showed a mastery of his ancestral language and asked, "Do you mean Dirty or star? The meaning is different with a high-pitched start to the word."

"Ford repeated the word pitched higher at the beginning.

"Dirty then?" said Jason.

Ford said, "Yes, but that does not mean we'll play dirty. Right?"

"Correct, sir," said Jason.

"You will fly to Bogota on Monday morning." Ford said, "and stay at Hotel Dorado Ferial Monday night. It is close to the airport."

"Your cover story is that you are a young married couple trying to learn more about historic central American sites for your university. Do not arouse suspicion. It is up to you to sort out sleeping arrangements. Make sure the double bed looks like they have slept in it. On Tuesday morning, a car will pick you up and take you to Puerto Arango. We booked you into a local hotel, the San Juan Apartments. It is important to keep the cover story. The airfield is south of the town. From there, a low-flying chopper will take you at night to your drop-off point, 20 miles short of your target. You'll travel by foot the rest of the way. We will keep a watch on your position via a satellite link. The rest of your team will arrive in a few days."

"Your instructions are to find, watch, and await further orders. Do not engage. We need to understand how cocaine gets here. They found a cryptic message underneath the body of a known associate of El Fantasma in a room at the local Marriott Hotel. "

"The cryptologists in the office must like us, but it will give us something to work on whilst on our honeymoon," Cora said with a laugh that whets Jason's appetite for what he hoped may come later.

Jason received the flight tickets delivered by the courier and drove the short distance from his apartment in North Miami to the airport well before the departure time. They had booked him and Cora on to the 10:50 direct flight to Bogota. They agreed to meet outside Starbucks. He waited in line to get a drink. A soft hand clasped his. There was no need to glance sideways; he knew it was Cora. With hot chocolates in hand, they moved together to await their flight.

Seated opposite Cora, Jason took in the vision before him. She wore light-weight pants, open-toed slip-on shoes, all topped off with a figure-hugging, pink chiffon blouse.

Cora's blonde hair flowed in gentle waves, stressing her glossy pink lips that were smiling at him. Jason's heart skipped a beat. Christmas day came in a single moment.

"Where have you been all my life?"

"Easy, tiger, we must follow the script. Our roles are to be newlyweds. We are just actors on the stage. It is not real," said Cora.

Jason wondered how Cora could keep a loving smile directed towards him yet be so icy cold. She continued the act, stroking his hand, tilting her head as she whispered sweet nothings his way. Her acting confused him, but concluded she was being professional.

They arose and Cora slipped her arm into Jason's and leaned towards him. As they walked, she smiled at him as she spoke. To all watching they were newlyweds, they made their way towards the book-in desk. As they waited, Cora fingered the rings on her finger. The passenger service agent smiled as she realized they had married earlier that day; she congratulated them and expressed hope that they would enjoy their honeymoon.

With their baggage weighed, they took it from them, and the agent handed over their boarding passes. They thanked the agent and moved through the barrier toward security checking and customs.

They sat and waited for their flight announcement.

Jason glanced at Cora and noticed bits of confetti placed in her hair.

He reflected again on her professionalism and how it enhanced her natural beauty.

They settled into their seats on the plane. Moments after take-off, Cora had rested her head on Jason's shoulder. He relaxed and alternated between looking out of the window and watching

Cora breathe as she worked on the cryptic message she had hidden between pages of Vogue magazine.

CHAPTER 2

As he turned off his burner phone, a smirk crossed his face. Emiliano Alvarez said, "Money can buy you anything in this world." He said that he knew the Feds and the Drug Enforcement Agency were coming at dawn. "They are watching our place now. Everyone quick, down to the cellar and through the tunnel, remember my bags. I don't want them to have my money."

Alvarez led his men to the cellar, moved the boxes hiding the entrance to the tunnel, turned on the lashed-up lights, and clambered along the tunnel, breathing in the stale, damp air. They pushed the door open after they arrived at the club.

"Oto," cried Alvarez, "watch the CCTV, and as soon as the feds find the tunnel entrance, blow the charges to block it, then get clear with Florez and Juan. 20K here to help make your way to Barba's farm. You all have the address in the text message I sent out. Keep it safe. We don't want those idiots from the DEA working it out." Alvarez continued, "The rest of you collect your money as you disperse and do likewise. Tomaz, Claudio, and Dolfo, with me."

With a quick exit by the backdoor, Alvarez and his close associates climbed into a waiting car and drove off under the speed limit so as not to raise suspicion.

"We need to leave these overrated police states. We can run our operations from another country and let others take the risks for us." barked Alvarez. "Pass me the bag with the blue stripe," he instructed.

On opening the bag, he removed several forged passports and handed them to the others. "Remember your alternative names. They aren't too bad. Mine is Juan Diaz; but I prefer the nickname the feds have for me, El Fantasma — The Ghost."

The group headed towards west on the 41 towards Marco Island.

Alvarez said, "Tomaz, keep to the speed limits. We don't want to be stopped.

Two hours later, whilst it was still dark the four of them arrived at the empty lot in Ember Ct on Smokehouse Creek, where a large, fast, catamaran awaited fueled and ready, a Thunder Cat capable of speeds over 120 miles per hour and if needed, should be able to outrun any Custom Patrol boat with speed and movability, but what Alvarez wanted was a quiet, unobtrusive trip to the edge of the US coastal waters where another boat awaited to head across the Gulf towards the Yucatan and relative safety.

He wasn't comfortable crossing from the Thunder Cat to the Sports Cruiser. He fell asleep after moving to a small cabin. The rest of the crew either laid out somewhere or watched as the false

Blue Merlin gear moved in harmony with the gentle waves as they traveled southwest, keeping outside the Cuban waters. "Tomaz, did you send Dolfo a message from me?" asked Alvarez. Tomaz nodded in a sleepy response. Time ambled as they voyaged, and all four succumbed to heavy eyelids.

Their trip was uneventful, and they roused Alvarez about ten miles off the Puerto coastline. He made use of the boat's satellite phone and called Dolfo. Dolfo confirmed the receipt of the message, and he understood it. Alvarez directed a powered inflatable to be lowered into the water. They climbed aboard, cast off, and cut through the waves towards the mainland. He knew where he wanted to land. Between the two properties he already owned, he directed towards the scrubland. Met by others, Alvarez took them all inside the house with the swimming pool.

The waiting staff had prepared a late breakfast meal for them. After simple pleasantries, Alvarez retired to his bedroom, opened a wardrobe, and took out his swimming trunks, changed, and draped a dressing gown over his shoulders before making his way out to the pool.

A bevy of adolescent dreams greeted him, all eager to please their famous boss. The Ghost took his place on a lounger as one girl placed a cool drink beside him and another poured suntan lotion onto his torso.

A young brunette he had never seen before removed the sunblock cream from the other girl and coated his legs with it. As she neared his trunks, Alvarez got hold of the girl's hand and said, "wait for me." With his robe discarded, he dived into the cool water and swam two lengths, then climbed out. He approached the same young girl, and taking by the hand he asked, "what is your name, honey?"

"Ana Torres," the girl replied.

"Well Ana Torres, you come with me and finish what you started." said Alvarez with a smile.

"Dolfo," he called, "Make sure I'm not disturbed." He and Ana spent the rest of the day and night inside the house.

At two o'clock, Ana slid from the bed and crept into the bathroom. She removed the back of the bathroom cabinet, exposing a phone, which connected to a pre-programmed number and sent a text message, "Ghost arrived."

She replaced the phone, wrapped the sim card in toilet tissue, snapped it, and flushed it down the toilet. After making sure it had gone, she returned to the bed, snuggling back up beside Alvarez.

Alvarez slipped from the bed, leaving the sleeping Ana. He sat down at the breakfast table and scraped butter over fresh toast. Tomaz walked up to Alvarez and presented him with the broken sim card which Ana had disposed of. "You were right to have that filter trap placed in the macerator sewer pipe," said Tomaz. "Someone flushed it down the toilet after midnight. We found it this morning after seeing the switch had tripped."

"That filter? Who knew about it?" asked Alvarez.

"Everyone except the new girl, Ana Torres." replied Tomaz.

"Pass me yours," said Alvarez, pointing to Tomaz's shoulder holster.

Alvarez returned to his bedroom, sat beside Ana, and stroked her hair until she awoke. "Hello, my beauty," he whispered.

Ana smiled and lifted her head. Alvarez placed his arm behind Ana's head, still smiling at her. He put the gun beneath her jaw and said, "Such a waste." Before Ana could become aware and plead for her life, he pulled the trigger.

"Tomaz, get this mess cleaned up," he snarled.

He returned to his breakfast after getting a fresh piece of toast. He scraped butter on it and bit into it. His eyes gazed at his coffee cup as he stirred it. Alvarez said, "We don't know whom she contacted. Let's get out of here."

Alvarez, Tomaz, Claudio, and Dolfo moved to the garage and climbed inside a black Mercedes.

The still sleeping, colorful town faded behind as they drove towards a waiting plane at a small airstrip five miles away.

They climbed aboard and the plane's twin engines roared to life. The plane flew into the air. They had a long journey ahead of them. Soon they were over open water again and heading towards the Nicaraguan coastline. Claudio knew where to land for extra fuel. He turned inland towards Kukrahill, a small coastal town. Next to the Catholic Church, there was a grass landing strip where fuel awaited. The four stretched their legs as others pumped and loaded the fuel.

Minutes later, they were airborne again, cutting across Costa Rica before crossing the open sea and turning east into Colombia, north of the Ecuador border.

"Tomaz, did you send the message?" asked Alvarez. Tomaz grunted an affirmative reply with his eyes closed.

In the fading light, they flew over the town of Pasto before they spotted the familiar Rio Caquetá. The plan followed the river east towards their goal, a hidden airstrip near Barba's farm. Tomaz phoned again about their imminent arrival. This gave Barba time to move braziers from hiding. They lit up the airstrip and had a welcoming group assembled. On landing, Barba was embracing Alvarez and kissing him on the cheek.

"I got your message and prepared for your arrival," said Barba through dark, smiling lips.

"The rest of my most trusted men are en route in different ways. They should be here within a week." Said Alvarez.

"Good," responded Barba. "Did you have any trouble?"

"Nothing I couldn't handle," replied Alvarez. "We need to keep an eye out for the Drug Enforcement Agency. How are your difficulties with that construction company going? I heard that someone is putting a spanner in the works. Is that right?"

"The government has removed a friend from office and is making trouble. They think they can stop us by getting rid of one man. They are wrong. Many of my men have run away to the hills to frightened to fight." said Barba. "Let us talk tomorrow. You're tired from your long journey. I have arranged for a comfort girl to help you get to sleep. She is good and clean. Enjoy, my friend."

CHAPTER 3

Cora slept through the attendant's announcement to sit up and fasten seat belts. Jason roused her. She met his offer to help with a rebuff. Cora, remembering the script, thanked him and allowed Jason to help her, kissing him on the cheek to say thank you.

The landing was faultless and smooth, and their departure from the airport via customs was straightforward. Outside there was a shuttle bus to the hotel, which took just 20 minutes. After leaving the shuttle, they felt heat. The air was thick with fumes and left a horrid taste in their mouths.

Cora tugged at her blouse to release it from the wet flesh and leaned against Jason as he stopped at the reception desk. The man said they had a message. He passed a small envelope to Jason, who opened it and read aloud, "Dad arrived home, love Aaron." "Oh, that is good," he said with a smile as he squeezed Cora's hand.

They went to the bathroom. Turning on the taps, he whispered to Cora, "El Fantasma has arrived in the Yucatan. It won't take him long to be here in Colombia." Cora nodded, understanding.

"Do you wish to check out the Museo-del-Oro?"

"Is that the Museum of Golden artifacts you keep talking about?" asked Cora.

"It is," replied Jason.

Jason arranged for a taxi by phoning the reception, and they left their room to descend the staircase to the ground floor.

"Your taxi has just arrived, sir," said the doorman.

The doorman passed a message to a man hiding in the shadows.

They left the hotel, crossed the pavement, and entered the taxi.

"Museo-del-Oro por favor," said Jason to the driver.

Twenty minutes later, they arrived, paid the entrance fee, and toured the beautiful exhibits.

Jason gave Cora a running commentary as they stopped beside each lit artifact.

He knew his subject well. It concerned a history of his ancestors and pre-Hispanic metallurgy. He held Cora's attention well.

Time passed and soon the museum was closing. They emerged back into the last rays of daylight. Jason's alert eyes noticed the man that the doorman at the hotel gave a message to, standing close to an exhibit taking photos of him and Cora.

They made their way back towards the hotel arm-in-arm. They stopped by a well-frequented restaurant. Jason and Cora entered, welcomed by El maître, shown to a table, and presented with the menu but their hunger to lead the way.

"Grilled steak and two glasses of bottled water, please," said Jason.

"Coq au vin for me, please," said Cora.

The server disappeared to return with two small bottles of water and clean glasses.

Jason and Cora spent the evening in small talk, keeping off the real reason for their being in Colombia. Jason paid for their meal with his Amex card Amex card, Jason paid, and together they continued their walk back to the hotel.

Nodding to the doorman, they moved across the reception to the lift and traveled to their floor. In their room, Jason saw that someone had moved and opened their suitcases. They won't find anything inside there, he mused. They busied getting clothing ready for tomorrow whilst continuing the pretense as they spoke, just in case of hidden microphones.

Cora moved towards the shower, kicking off her shoes as she neared the door. She turned towards Jason and mouthed the word NO to him as he asked if she wanted company. After turning on the TV, he found the English Channel.

Cora emerged wrapped in a large towel that exposed her leg past her hip. Jason's eyes popped out! Pointing to the shower, Cora pointed out the shower was free. He entered, then stripped and stepped inside the shower tray and turned on the water. He yelped; Cora had turned the mixer valve to cold. Jason could hear her laughing from the bedroom as he turned the valve back to warm.

Before he emerged from the shower, she turned off the lights and TV. In the dim light, he could make out that Cora was already in bed.

He dropped his towel and pulled the covers down and moved closer to Cora. Cora had pre-empted his move and whilst he was in the shower, she had 'apple-pied' the bedding sideways. There was an impenetrable sheet and a pillow between them.

Thinking of what could have been, he fell asleep. Jason awoke in the early hours as he felt Cora leave the bed. He opened his eyes to catch sight of her disrobed body move across the room and open the window before getting back into bed. He knew that the play was about making out they slept together. Oh, it was so difficult.

When morning arrived, they awoke to discover that they had moved into the 'spoons in the draw' position. Cora leaned over and gathered her towel and wrapped it around herself before leaving the bed and going into the bathroom. Jason left the bed and slipped on fresh clothes whilst waiting for Cora. The bed looked like a honeymoon bed.

They had just finished breakfast when the reception sent a bellhop to let them know their car had arrived. Jason thanked the receptionist as he paid for the night with a wink. The receptionist acknowledged with a knowing grin.

Jason and Cora entered the waiting car. "G'morning, Mr. Balan," said the company driver, "I have something for you from Mr. Ford," as he passed a package over to Jason.

Inside, Jason found a note and a handgun. As he read the note, he took a deep breath. Ana was dead, shot in the head. He had liked Ana; they had been friends since the day they joined the agency together. Checking the clip was full, he placed it inside his pocket and handed the note to Cora. "Well, it looks like El Fantasma is working his way to Colombia," said Cora.

Jason did not answer. It filled him with anger at the loss of such a close friend.

Their journey to Puerto Arango was quiet, with few interruptions. Jason and Cora, no longer players on a stage, sat apart in the back seat.

They continued that way for over five hours when the driver broke the silence by saying. "We are about halfway. I know a good place to eat. I think we should stop there."

Jason mumbled an almost inaudible reply. They came to the outskirts of Aipo Verde, and the driver took them towards a clean eating place—Verde Restaurante. Back in the script, Cora moved across the seat and snuggled up beside Jason as the car parked beside the entrance.

It still filled Jason with thoughts of Ana when they sat down to eat. Cora ordered for them all, "Tres tortilla por favor."

The server asked "¿aqua mineral."

Jason mumbled a thanks.

With a struggle, Jason smiled at Cora, who smiled back. He had to remember that someone could watch them. He took Cora's hand and licked the juices that had run from the tortilla onto her fingers as she ate. Cora smiled at his action, took his hand, and kissed it. She knew how much he was hurting about Ana's death. She would hug him better once they got back to the car.

Before long, they arrived in Puerto Arango and found their hotel, the San Juan Apartmentos. The committed host greeted them and introduced them to his family.

Jason explained to the host that they were on a working honeymoon and they would leave early in the morning. He explained they had a long trip into the rainforest. He was keen to visit a discovered tierradentro—a hypogeum for his university.

Their host said he understood and wished them a good night as he pointed out a nearby restaurant.

They could see a bouquet on the bed when they opened the apartment door. The card with them read, "Enjoy, but be careful. Love Aaron."

They showered; Cora used an unscented soap. By asking why Cora gave a simple response, "Chanel No.5 is not a rainforest fragrance."

They dressed in camouflage coveralls and left the apartment. Their company driver was waiting. He took away their cases, replacing them with small rucks. They drove along a narrow dirt road. It took just moments to leave the town behind. A helicopter sat waiting as the driver went down a track.

No visible markings were visible on the helicopter. The pilot ushered them aboard and instructed them to put headpieces on. They would fly low, just over tree height. From the window in an hour they could see the Rio Caquet.

As the helicopter lifted off, the pilot pulled out his night sights. He switched the onboard transponder off. They followed the river over Curillo to the drop-off point. The pilot removed his night-sights and said, "Look ahead. That is Barba's landing strip lit up. They must expect someone special." Cora looked at Jason and said, "El

Fantasma." Jason nodded. The pilot put the chopper down in a tiny clearing beside the river. After wishing them good luck, he lifted off, heading back the way he came.

Jason and Cora had arrived much closer to the farm than they had expected. There was a track in the forest. They set off, keeping on the track, heading all the way to the farm. There was a distinct sound of a plane getting closer and lower. It was clear they were near to their quarry; Jason stopped and climbed a tree beside the path. He dropped a rope and assisted Cora in joining him. They pulled branches together and fixing them with a rope. They built a small platform for him and Cora to rest on.

It had become cold. They had to drape a camouflage oilskin around them and huddle together. Sleep followed for the couple.

CHAPTER 4

Jason woke with a start. Below, he could hear voices. He placed his hand over Cora's mouth and woke her. Her eyes stared at Jason, and she nodded to show she understood. The men were talking while they listened. They were getting away from Barba's farm to join others up in the hills. They were unwilling to go against the government agents. History had taught them; it was a folly as many of their associates had died trying the same.

Jason smiled and said, "Now that is interesting news."

At the farm, Barba had been trimming his bushy black beard when he received the news of more defections. His anger erupted. He kicked a chair so hard it flew across the room and crashed through the window. Awakened by the noise, Alvarez rushed into Barba's room with his pistol cocked and ready.

"Barba, what's going on?" he demanded.

Barba exclaimed, "My men are cowards."

He told Alvarez that the Colombian National Police (CNP) had been following novel ways, infiltrating drug cartels like his, and based on the intelligence gained, "They were ready every time we made a move against them."

"I have many loyal followers arriving soon," said Alvarez. "Let me lead your men and mine up into the hills and compel your defectors to return with me so we can plan out a strategy to go against the CNP."

"I like your thoughts," said Barba, creasing a smile across his face that lifted his beard. "Come, my friend, let me show you what has changed since you were last here."

The pair moved across the dirt to a large shed-like structure. Barba handed Alvarez a mask to wear. "I don't want you hooked on our product," he said.

Inside there were masked, naked women of various ages working and watched over by armed men. They were weighing out the white pills and filling pre-labeled bags.

"We bring the women from up north. We keep them gagged and blindfolded all the way; removing gags to feed them. I don't want local natives working here. They know too much, and anyway, we keep them happy buying coca leaves from them. As for these, once we finish with their services filling bags of our special product, we take them out into the forest many miles from here and dispose of them," said Barba.

"Come, see what little trick my chemists have invented."

Alvarez noted the air pressure inside was much higher in the next shed. It blew in clean air under pressure, preventing cocaine carried in the air from entering.

Barba offered a cocaine surface wipe test strip to Alvarez. "Pretend that you work for the CNP. Test the outside of the bag."

Alvarez removed the test kit from the foil and took the cap off. He wiped the prong across the bag. With care, he removed the cap from the buffer solution and placed the prong into the solution for 15 seconds. He fitted the cap and laid the kit flat for 10 minutes.

It surprised him to see the T (test line) present. Negative—no cocaine on the sample.

"Amazing," said Alvarez, "you have circumvented the CNP's first line of defense against our product. How did you do it?"

With his broad grin shining through his beard, Barba said, "It's down to my chemists. They created a method to coat the bags."

The pair watched as the bags arrived from the bagging shed, and seal checking takes place. They sprayed the bags with something from cans. The cans had the labels covered. It turned traces of powder into mush to be wiped clean. We place the bags into a bath of sweet-smelling ingredients. They leave the outside of the bag to dry, turning every few minutes before the same wipe test is done. They returned any failures to follow the process again.

"That is very interesting. What are you using on the bags?" said Alvarez.

"Would you believe it's WD40? The bath has special solvents and hair conditioner in it," said Barba. "Come, let me show you to the other sheds."

They left and moved to a noisy shed. "Our growers bring the coca leaves here in large sacks. We are trying to chop them with industrial shredding machines. It seems to work well. We dust the chopped leaves with lime and add a little water before putting them into the leaf mulcher." Barba continued, "The mulch gets transferred to one of the washing machines we have adapted for the purpose, then kerosene gets added."

"The machines work nonstop for two days to remove wax from the leaves. To get rid of the waste vegetation, we filter it again. The liquid is mixed with acid to separate it from cocaine sulfate. That is then mixed with caustic soda to kill off the acid. At the end you get a gummy, brown-yellow paste." he said, pointing to containers full of the stuff.

"We dissolve the coca paste into more sulfuric acid with potassium permanganate added. That gets rid of the impurities in the paste, and it changes to a faint white color," said Barba.

Alvarez said. "I have only dealt with the finished product and not its production."

Barba continued, "Filtering the colorless solution and treating it with ammonia to kill off the last of the sulfuric acid. we get pure cocaine hydrochloride. The dried powder gets put in the Chinese pill-making machine, pressed into various shapes, then packaged as you saw in the other shed. We only distribute pure cocaine. We let others grind the pills back to powder and cut that with talcum powder or baking soda. There you are, my friend, my farm in all its glory."

"I thought you had workers treading out the leaves." Said Alvarez.

"I have solar panels now to charge batteries and run the machines." said Barba. "I can produce more in less time with automated machines."

The pair wandered back to Barba's house and seated themselves down beside the fan to get relief from the sticky heat. "Water," he shouted, and Barba's wife entered and gave them two sealed bottles of mineral water.

"Thank you, Blanca," said Barba. Turning to Alvarez, he asked, "Do you remember this beauty? I married her last year. I know she is only 17 years old, but she helps keep me young. Don't you, my love?"

Blanca smiled back, and looking at Alvarez, she said, "I'm not sure I remember you."

"I can only remember you as a little shoeless girl," said Alvarez, "but you have grown into an exquisite young lady."

Blanca blushed and left the two men free to talk about defections.

"Barba," said Alvarez, "give me the command over your men and once my men arrive, we will combine forces and follow the traitors into the hills and compel them to return."

"That sounds good to me. I will tell them you are my number two. They will obey you as if it was me giving the orders," said Barba.

They spent the rest of the day just chatting and reminiscing about times long since gone. As they sat at the table for dinner, Alvarez's satellite phone burst into life.

"Boss, are you there?"

He recognized the voice. "Hi Florez, where are you now? Any trouble?" Alvarez asked.

"No problems. We are in Colombia. I told them to keep in small groups so they wouldn't draw attention. We will be with you soon. Over."

"Superb. Barba just whispered to me he will arrange a bit of comfort for you when you get here. He put the phone down.

"Pedro, get in here," called Barba.

"Yes boss," said Pedro.

Barba looked right at him and said, "Pedro, Alvarez and I have combined forces. I am making him my number two."

Pedro's face filled with anger; his eyes were like fire. "You promised me that role!" he shouted.

"Calm down. You won't lose any money. I made you rich, and I will make you richer yet. Alvarez has a lot of loyal men under his command. We need them to help us. Our gangs will make a force that the CNP can't deal with.

Pedro agreed to the instruction, even though he wasn't sure he liked it. The camp was still asleep as the Alvarez and Pedro met.

"Tomaz, I need to know for sure. Do you trust me?" asked Alvarez.

"Yeah, you know I do," said Tomaz.

"I have to ask you something kind of special. Will you vow to do as I say and never reveal it?" said Alvarez.

Tomaz confirmed he would.

"Good, then I will make you my number two. Come for a walk in the forest. I want to speak away from here."

They walked over to a narrow pathway and continued their conversation, stopping beneath where Jason and Cora lay secreted on the treetop.

"Are you getting this?" whispered Jason.

"I sure am," replied Cora.

"When they go, I'll call it in. We need to see where this leads. We shouldn't flood the area with other operatives."

Alvarez and Tomaz moved away and out of earshot; Jason called Ford to appraise him of events. Jason and Cora made their tree-top nest more camouflaged, secure, and weatherproof, knowing they could be there for a long time.

They considered their difficulties regarding food. They needed a source of regular supply because they only had a few days of food.

"I'll check out the back of the camp. I'll see what I can find," whispered Jason as he checked all was clear.

On the ground, he started moving around the edge of the farm. He slipped in and out of the forest cover. Jason tried doors after listening for sounds coming from the huts before moving to the next one. As he approached one hut, he could hear the voices of women speaking in a language he recognized as Mayan. He learned that someone had kidnapped them and brought them down to the farm to fill the bags with cocaine pills.

Jason tapped on a window and called to the women in Mayan. The hut was now silent as Jason spoke again. A window opened at the rear of the hut and Jason moved to converse with a naked black-haired woman in braids he assumed to be their leader.

"Please don't call out," he pleaded as he brushed bees away, "my name is Jason Balan. I came to see what was happening. I want to get you home."

"How do you know our language?" asked an older woman.

"My ancestors were Maya, and my parents taught me," replied Jason.

"Your last name helps me understand that." She asked if he knew what it meant.

Jason replied that, "Balan is Yucatec Maya for jaguar, a spirit of security and night protection; and I try to act like one as I pursue my quarry and bring safety to the innocent. From a place of cover, we have observed you in this hut for days. We now need your help; my colleague and I need food and water as we work out a plan of action."

The woman replied with a smile. "Let us help. My name is Xochil."

"Ah, I can see why you have that name. You are a flower," said Jason.

He continued, "If you could bring food and water to the small path near the river, just a little way along the path you will see a Marmalade Bush with light orange flowers beside the base of a tree, hide the food behind the tree, we will collect it when safe to do so."

"I know that bush," said a voice.

"Would you like something now?" asked Xochil.

"That would be wonderful," said Jason

He slipped back away from the hut and into the edge of the forest to conceal himself and wait as the women busied themselves gathering foodstuffs. The window opened, and they lowered a woven carrier bag filled with food. Jason moved to collect it and disappeared into the forest after thanking the ladies.

Cora had seen Jason move back into the forest. She lowered the rope once Jason was at the foot of the tree. Jason arrived and attached the carrier bag to the rope, and Cora started lifting it when she heard voices and stopped pulling the carrier up. He heard the men and hid. The voices drifted away. She assumed all was OK and completed the lift. The contents pleased her. She lowered the rope again, and Jason joined her.

CHAPTER 5

Two men met at night.

"Tomaz, I need to know for sure. Do you trust me?" asked Alvarez.

"Yeah, you know I do," said Tomaz.

"I have to ask you something kind of special, then. Will you vow to do as I say and never reveal it?" said Alvarez.

Tomaz confirmed he would.

"Good, then I will make you my number two. Come for a walk in the forest. I want to speak away from here."

They walked over to a narrow pathway and continued their conversation, stopping beneath where Jason and Cora lay secreted on the treetop.

"Are you getting this?" whispered Jason.

"I sure am," replied Cora.

"When they go, I'll call it in. We need to see where this leads. We don't need to flood the area with operatives."

Alvarez and Tomaz moved away and out of earshot; Jason called Ford to appraise him of events. Jason and Cora made their tree-top nest more camouflaged, secure, and weatherproof, knowing they could be there for a long time.

The pair needed a regular supply of food. They only had enough for a few days.

"I'll scout to see what I can find," whispered Jason as he checked all was clear.

He slipped out of cover as he moved around the farm. Jason tried doors after listening for sounds coming from the huts before moving to the next one. As he approached one hut, he could hear the voices of women speaking in a language he recognized as Mayan. He learned that someone had kidnapped them and brought them down to the farm to fill the bags with cocaine pills.

Jason tapped on a window and called to the women in Mayan. The hut was now silent as Jason spoke again. A window opened at the rear of the hut and Jason moved to converse with a naked black-haired woman in braids he assumed to be their leader.

"Please don't call out," he pleaded as he brushed bees away, "my name is Jason Balan. I came here to see what Barba was up to. Can you help me get you back home and away from this hellhole?"

"How do you know our language?" asked an older woman.

"My ancestors were Maya, and my parents taught me," replied Jason.

"Your last name helps me understand that." The woman asked what it meant.

Jason replied that, "Balan is Yucatec Maya for jaguar, a spirit of security and night protection; and I try to act like one as I pursue my quarry and bring safety to the innocent. From a place of cover, we have observed you in this hut for days. We now need your help; my colleague and I need food and water as we work out a plan of action."

The woman replied with a smile. "We're happy to help. We have enough. My name is Xochil."

"Ah, I can see why you have that name. You are a flower," said Jason.

He continued, "If you could bring food and water to the small path near the river, just a little way along the path you will see a Marmalade Bush with light orange flowers beside the base of a tree, hide the food behind the tree, we will collect it when safe to do so."

A female said she knew that bush. "Do you want us to help you out?"

"That would be wonderful," said Jason

He slipped back away from the hut and into the edge of the forest to conceal himself and wait as the women busied themselves gathering foodstuffs. The window opened, and they lowered a woven carrier bag filled with food. Jason moved to collect it and disappeared into the forest after thanking the ladies.

Cora had seen Jason move back into the forest. She prepared herself to lower the rope once he was at the foot of the tree. Jason arrived and attached the carrier bag to the rope, and Cora started lifting it when she heard voices. She stopped pulling the carrier up, thinking that she had heard the men. Jason had heard them and hid. The men moved across the open center of the camp, and voices faded. She completed the lift; the contents pleased her. She lowered the rope again, and soon Jason joined her.

They had used the rope every nighttime to deal with toileting needs, but they both needed to bathe. As Cora had pointed out, Jason was getting to smell rich!

The pair sat monitoring the farm as they made notes and ate the fresh food prepared for them by Xochil and her associates. As dusk fell, they could see the guards and workers getting ready to eat. It is the best time to enter the river.

Jason kept guard as Cora slipped out of her camouflage suit and into her sports bra and briefs. She slipped into the river hidden beneath overhanging branches and freshened herself with an insignificant movement of surface water. Without warning, Cora was waving her arms. Jason had been waiting for Cora, now he knew something had disturbed her, and he rushed to her aid. Jason helped her from the river and listened to her desperate pleas for help. She was hopping on the spot and pointing to her briefs. Something had slipped into them, and she was begging for help.

"Get it out, get it out," Cora implored. "I don't know what it is."

Jason moved close and lowered Cora's briefs to see a small fish flapping about, colored a striking blue and red. "It's OK, it is a Cardinal Tetra, not a Piranha." He said, grinning.

"You can stop smirking now." said an embarrassed Cora.

"You're welcome. Anytime." replied a chuckling Jason as he stripped to lower himself into the river.

Jason dressed and returned to their tree house to find Cora speaking with Aaron Ford.

"Agent Ford wants us to wait, then follow the dissidents from the farm and report on what they are doing." said a blushing Cora. "He also asked if we had got anywhere with that code. I told him no. We are still trying to figure it out."

CHAPTER 6

The sound of heavy trucks arriving in the compound awakened Jason and Cora, followed by much shouting and laughter. "The rest of Alvarez's team has arrived," said Jason as he scanned the compound with night sights.

"We need to know their plans," said Jason as he readied himself to slip down the rope. He crept around the farm until he was behind a large hut. He could hear the proceedings in the compound.

After greeting his men, Alvarez took them to the empty hut. Jason listened as Alvarez spoke. "Barba and I plan to join forces and go up into the mountain, and persuade his dissenters to return and go with us against the local Government rats that have interfered with farm production."

"I will remain here with a skeleton crew to maintain production," interrupted Barba.

"Barba had two men follow them. They reported back their probable location," said Alvarez. "They will lead us. Rest up, for now. We must walk a long way. We will begin our journey in the morning."

Jason returned to the waiting Cora and told her of Alvarez's plans. They gathered up the supplies Xochil had given them, placing them into rucks. "We need to rest and be ready to follow them through the forest.

In the morning, Cora and Jason could see a large body of men assembled, kitted out, and ready to travel towards their goal. Their route followed the path to where Jason and Cora sat secreted.

After advising the women workers about their plans. The pair left the camp behind and were soon in thick rain forests. Jason and Cora followed the crowd at a safe distance, listening to the constant sound of chatter.

At nightfall, Jason and Cora crept around Alvarez's camp, keeping hidden in the forest, moving forward on the path to know when Alvarez continued the journey.

Secreted near the path, Cora and Jason sat down to eat the food Xochil had provided. After eating, they wrapped themselves together in a camouflaged waterproof sheet.

With undergrowth pulled around them for security, they snuggled down for warmth and sleep.

"STOP IT," said Cora as she nudged Jason in the ribs. "I said no."

Jason asked, "What are you on about?"

"It is you. What are you doing?" replied Cora as she pulled the camouflaged sheet off them and turned on her torch.

"Eek!" cried Cora as she saw a snake sliding between her legs. "I thought you were making a move on me."

Another snigger escaped Jason. "You'd be so lucky," he said as he laughed. "It is a Rainbow Boa. Don't worry, it's not poisonous. They kill their prey by constriction."

"I don't care, get it off me," said a shuddering Cora.

Jason grabbed the snake by the tail and threw it towards a distant tree. "Can we get some sleep now?

"Another one might crawl up my trouser leg," pleaded a frightened Cora.

"Keep your boots on, tuck the trouser legs inside your boots and tie the boots around the trouser legs. Put the tunic top into your trouser waistband with the tunic done up to the neck. Put your hat on with the straps behind your ears and under your chin. To make sure no creepy crawlies get in tomorrow's socks, pull them on over your boots, not inside. Didn't you listen to any of the jungle advice?" Jason asked with a touch of sarcasm, and continued, "I thought you were supposed to be my intelligence specialist."

Cora ignored his comment and asked if she could get closer to him, just for added safety.

"Now go to sleep. We have a long walk ahead of us tomorrow." Instructed Jason, smirking in the dark.

Dawn was breaking as Cora again was nudging Jason in the ribs.

"For pity's sake," said Jason, "now what?"

Cora pointed to her forehead, powerless to speak from fear. She was looking at a green frog with bright red eyes. Cora's eyes crossed while looking upwards. They were looking at each other.

"Is it a poison dart-frog?" pleaded Cora.

"No, it's a tree frog, but I will show you one later in the day if you stop waking me up."

Cora knocked the frog off her head and cuddled up against Jason even tighter. Sleep was far from her mind. Every sound seemed amplified. She was certain all of creation would be her companion if she slept. She was on the forest floor and she thought everything would get her.

After a sleepless night, she went to see her personal needs in the forest. When she returned, Jason had gathered and repacked their things into the rucks, leaving out a machete.

They sat and waited for Alvarez and his gang to pass by, then followed again, keeping a respectful distance between them and the noisy mob ahead.

Jason kept a good lookout for those ahead whilst scanning the forest's edge for bamboo. He had spotted one, and cut down a long cane with one stroke and trimmed off the ends and node growths as he walked.

The group ahead had stopped. They had paused for lunch. They slipped back to the forest edge and also snacked. Jason found a fallen tree and Cora could see as he placed the bamboo across it and rolled it beneath the sharp machete just above a node. In minutes, he had cut through the internode. Turning to the bamboo's other end, he focused his attention on the next node. With the same rolling of the bamboo beneath his machete, he cut through it and produced a perfect tube about 15 inches long.

He repeated working on another, wider piece of bamboo, only to leave one end sealed. He placed both bamboo pieces in his ruck and readied himself to continue following Alvarez.

She asked why he did it.

"You'll see later," came the answer.

The path they followed moved towards a small river. Jason and Cora moved near the edge of the forest for concealment. Progress was slow, and Alvarez was moving ahead all the time.

"We will have to keep a sharper lookout and follow the path and duck back in the forest as soon as we catch sight of them," said Jason.

The pair picked up the pace and soon saw Alvarez ahead. They dropped back into the forest. They continued in this vogue until it neared dusk and Alvarez's gang stopped for the night. Jason and Cora moved inside the forest's edge. They took a wide berth around the gang to get in front. Ready for the next day's walk. They cleared a patch of ground of all debris, spread out one sheet, and sat down to eat. Before settling down to sleep, Jason rose and collected an open seedpod from a nearby Kapok tree, putting it inside his rucks.

Cora had followed Jason's earlier instructions and secured herself within her clothes. Jason gathered foliage to cover themselves with after the top sheet was over them. Hidden and camouflaged, they slept close to each other for warmth and comfort. Dawn arrived, and Cora continued to sleep. Jason left her and traveled deeper into the forest to deal with personal needs. On his return, he spotted a Bougain Villea plant. With great care, he removed several sharp thorns. With care, he returned, still holding the thorns to where Cora still lay sleeping. He woke her, then busied himself as she tended to her personal needs. On her return, they ate a simple meal and waited for Alvarez to pass by.

They realized something wasn't right after a while. Alvarez and his gang never arrived. Jason was worried that the group had crossed the river and that they might lose them. With care not to disclose their position, they backtracked to where the gang had stayed overnight. All had left. At the water's edge, Jason and Cora could see where the bank was wet from water splashes. They slid into the water and waded across.

"Watch out for piranhas and cardinal tetras," joked Jason with a huge grin on his face.

It was obvious where Alvarez had climbed out; the bank was wet from the many bodies that had followed him.

They found the path after leaving the river that Alvarez and his gang had taken. Jason and Cora picked up the pace to catch up with them.

By midday, the forest was thinning out, and the path was getting steep. Vegetation was giving way to rocks. Ahead of them, they could see a wisp of smoke. Alvarez had stopped for the day. Through his scopes, he saw that above where Alvarez camped, there was a secluded location with several trees and other vegetation set into the mountainside.

"I guess that is where the dissidents holed up," said Jason as he passed the scopes to Cora.

"Cora, call Agent Ford and appraise him of the situation. I'm going to watch the other camp. Keep yourself hidden. Rest up and wait for my return. Do nothing. Do you understand?" instructed Jason. "Nothing!"

CHAPTER 7

Jason moved around Alvarez's camp and ascended towards the dissident's hideout. He stopped near the ridge that protected the camp. Through his night sights, he could see guards placed to warn the camp of those approaching. He turned around and looked at Alvarez's campsite. He spotted two bodies engaged in conversation. Without noise, he moved closer to hear what they were saying.

"Tomaz," said Alvarez, "I want you to climb up and ask their leader to come down and speak with me."

"OK," said Tomaz, who then set off, following the path towards the camp.

Jason made himself comfortable and waited for Tomaz to return and report.

"Alvarez," said Tomaz, "their leader is a man called Nazeef. He said he has no intentions of coming down to speak with you. He doesn't trust you."

"Go up again and tell him to bring his guards with him if it frightens him," said Alvarez.

Tomaz climbed towards the camp, only to report back ten minutes later.

"He still won't come," said Tomaz.

"I'm going to see him alone. Said Alvarez.

Jason, keeping away from the path, kept pace with Alvarez as he moved towards the ridge. Through his night scopes, he could see the two men coming together. He moved closer to listen to their conversation.

"I'm the leader of the men below. My name is Alvarez. Are you Nazeef?"

"That is correct. What do you want?"

"If you make me your number two, I will help you capture those below and we will go against Barba together," said Alvarez.

"That is not possible," said Nazeef.

Alvarez replied, "I have a trusted man giving out many bottles of aguardiente for the men to drink, celebrating their arrival at your encampment, and the prospect of capturing you and taking you all back to Barba for punishment." "This is my plan. Your men will surround my men when they fall into a drunken slumber. In the morning, Tomaz and I will convince them to surrender and join you in returning to Barba's farm."

Nazeef said. "I will tell my men that you are my number two, and together we will attack Barba in force."

Jason watched as Alvarez followed the path towards his camp, and he returned to Cora to inform her of Alvarez's plan. They moved a greater distance away and, once secreted, took turns to watch and await events unfold in the morning.

Just before dawn, Nazeef's men descended the path and encircled Alvarez's men, and waited for them to awake. Alvarez's men arose as a sharp realization hit them. The Nazeef's men were in control of them. Death was certain. They pleaded with Alvarez to surrender. At their request, he spoke with Nazeef, and both agreed to the wishes of the men and combined their forces. With the aguardiente that remained, they celebrated their union.

By half-past nine in the morning, the group had begun their trip back to Barba's camp. Jason and Cora checked out Nazeef's old camp, foraging for food to sustain them on their return.

They found a large amount of left food stuff and gleaned what they could carry and began the return journey after appraising Agent Ford of Alvarez's plans by satellite phone.

As before, they followed at a safe distance, keeping themselves hidden.

They needed to arrive at the river before them. Their pace increased, and they overtook Nazeef and Alvarez to arrive at the river first.

Jason and Claire moved downstream from the place that Alvarez had used earlier. They slipped into the water so as not to splash the bank and crossed, leaving the river through a reed patch to hide their passage, and proceeded to where Alvarez had camped. The pair removed a short distance from it and hid up, waiting.

A very noisy band of followers declared the imminent arrival of Alvarez and the others. Jason and Cora watched as they settled down for the night and noticed Alvarez and Tomaz slide away from the group towards where they lay hidden. Just a few feet from their hiding place, they watched the conversation.

"Tomaz, I want you to place these thorns around Nazeef whilst he sleeps so that at least one of them will scratch him. Be careful, I coated them with the secretions of the golden frog. I don't want you injured. When he reacts to the poison, rush to his aid and kick the thorns into the undergrowth." said Alvarez.

Tomaz agreed and slipped off to conduct the deadly plan.

At dawn, they could hear a loud hubbub coming from the camp. They could not rouse Nazeef. Tomaz proceeded to his body, flicked away the placed thorns, and tried to resuscitate him before Alvarez arrived. Superstition trumped reason. One of the gang members claimed to have seen a very large black butterfly, a harbinger of death, land on Nazeef as he slept. They concluded he must have been evil and had his soul carried away. They lay his body to rest in a shallow grave covered with old vegetation. Alvarez, as the second in charge, became the leader and chose Tomaz as his deputy. Alvarez then instructed the men to continue their journey toward Barba's farm.

The pair followed the path ahead of the group. Jason and Cora arrived at the next campsite. They hid and waited for the group to return. Once more noise from the group declared their imminent arrival.

As the group sat down to eat, they watched as Alvarez and Tomaz moved away from the group and spoke. They couldn't hear or know their plans, but they saw Tomaz depart along the path. After calling Agent Ford to tell him of their observations, they settled down for the night.

Before morning light, Jason and Cora had re-joined the path and were making good progress when they spotted Tomaz and Barba hurrying along the path. They remained hidden in the vegetation as Tomaz and Barba passed them by. Whilst keeping a safe distance back, they followed them and watched as Pedro, Barba's former number two, ran to greet them. No sooner than he did, Tomaz stabbed Barba in the heart and ran after Pedro, crying out loud that he had killed Barba. Tomaz caught the man and slit his throat, shouting out that he had caught the murderer. Alvarez and the others arrived at the scene of carnage and praised Tomaz for his heroism in capturing the culprit.

Alvarez slapped Tomaz on the back and said, "well done, my faithful friend. I will reward you."

Amazed at the deceit they had witnessed, they moved away from the scene and back into the forest to inform Agent Ford.

A few hours later, Jason and Cora watched from their tree house as Alvarez arrived with the entire gang; they took Barba and Pedro's corpses into the center of the compound. Through tear-filled eyes,

Blanca thanked Tomaz that Barba's murderer was dead. "I knew he was angry with Barba and jealous of you," said Blanca. Alvarez comforted the grieving widow and moved off towards Barba's old hut with her.

Jason pointed out the obvious to Cora that Alvarez, by murder and deception, now controlled the whole of Barba's farm, export routes, and production plant, together with the distribution facilities in the USA.

With the men otherwise engaged, Cora thought it was secure enough to freshen up. As she moved beside the marmalade bush, a gang member who had been seeing to his ablutions caught hold of her and, whilst shouting, dragged her off into the compound screaming.

CHAPTER 8

Cora pleaded she had got lost after being separated from her husband, who was researching pre-Hispanic metallurgy at a discovered tierradentro—a hypogeum for his university.

She continued to explain that they had been near a town called Curillo beside the Rio Caquetá. She lost her way back to the camp after visiting the Pentecostal church.

"I think I took a wrong turn at a junction in the path." Said a desperate Cora. "I tried to backtrack, but that made things worse. The last two nights I slept on the ground. I am tired, scared, and want to go back to my husband. Please help me."

"She wants her husband," laughed Alvarez, to the amusement of the others. "Lock her up with the other women while we check out her story. She could make us some money. Maybe give us a treat on a chilly night."

Jason watched on from the treehouse. Cora remembered the story. He called Ford and asked that he speak with the contact in Curillo and arrange for a police search for Cora beside the river to the southeast of the town.

Alvarez had Cora placed with the Maya women and locked the door. The women gathered around her; it was easy for the women to guess that she was Jason's partner.

Xochil made herself known to Cora. They embraced like long-lost sisters. Cora told them they would help and that they should wait.

He could do nothing to help Cora from where he was. He waited until the camp was quiet, then traced his steps back to the women's hut, tapped on a window, and waited for a reply. A window opened and Xochil stood there.

"Don't worry she said, she is here safe and well. Would you like to speak to her?"

Jason confirmed he would, and Cora appeared at the window.

"Cora, I have spoken with Agent Ford. The police are searching for you. So, if Alvarez checks the story, it will hold up," said Jason.

"Have you any ideas yet?" asked Cora

"I'm working on something," said Jason as he noticed three golden frogs at the edge of the forest. "I must get back and keep watch."

After the women gave him some food, he went back into the forest.

Cora was beautiful, an issue not missed by Alvarez and the gang. He must act, but how?

Jason ate and saw that the coast was clear. He descended from the tree and headed to the hut that

Blanca had entered. As he stood beside an opened window, he could hear Blanca explain the routes that Barba had used to ship cocaine to the USA. A shipment had just left the farm. They were almost ready to arrange another shipment that will fill the boat. He flicked a bee away and crept back to the treehouse to tell Ford. Jason asked that his team in Bogota to be sent down to assist him in evacuating the women.

As he rested up, he recalled the time he played lacrosse at university. He rose with a start. Now he had a plan. The last hut to open was the ladies' hut. That would give him about 15 minutes to act from when the men finished their breakfast and gathered in the compound center. Without a sound, he busied himself making a wooden lacrosse stick.

Before the first light, he tapped on the ladies' window and told Xochil to keep the ladies inside the hut when they hear shouting after the men's breakfast. With Cora's help, they must climb out of the window. Circle around the compound to the parked trucks, and drive back along the dirt road, to where the rest of Jason's team waited to take them back to safety.

After slipping back into the forest, he waited for the sun to rise. Jason drew the bamboo tube he had fashioned from his pocket, along with the thorns held in the closed tube. With care, he wrapped seedpod cotton around the ends of the thorns, securing it with a thin thread from a long leaf plant, and laid them side-by-side. Last night, he had noticed three golden frogs beside an urn plant. He tipped the urn plant sideways and out came the three frogs. With care not to touch them, he rubbed each thorn point across their backs. Then placed the darts point down in the bamboo quiver.

He made his way to the storage hut near where washing machines made a constant drone.

On entering the hut, Jason discovered the usual ingredients for making cocaine: sulfuric acid, potassium permanganate, and kerosene.

Chemistry and physics were subjects he loved at college and university. With that knowledge, he devised a plan to create a disturbance and concern in the camp.

He spread a large quantity of potassium permanganate across the wooden floor and poured sulfuric acid on it, mixing the two with a broom.

An old plastic five-gallon container cut into a scoop left on the floor attracted his attention. Jason fixed it to hang over the edge of a workbench held in place by a leaf thread to stop it from falling. Above this, he placed a container of kerosene. With the kerosene container opened, it would dribble into the scoop; when the scoop was full, it would topple, breaking the leaf thread and pouring its contents onto the mix below—instant fire!

He then carried the ingredients to the battery hut, the filling and sealing huts, where he contrived the same incendiary devices.

Things in the food hut were getting noisy, and Jason assumed the gang was about to leave for the compound, he opened the diesel container's screw lid leaving a gentle flow into the scoop in the first hut, then went from hut to hut doing the same.

He arrived back beside the ladies' hut as the food hut door opened. The men poured out into the compound. Alvarez planned to give them instructions for the day. Jason readied himself beneath a hanging bee's nest at the forest's edge with his homemade lacrosse stick. As Alvarez opened his mouth to speak. Jason caught hold of the nest and hurled it to the compound center. Total pandemonium followed; the men were rushing around, trying to get rid of furious bees intent on attacking their assumed enemy. The bare-chested men were easy targets for the bees. Jason assisted the bees with poison darts.

Everyone ran to the river to escape the bees. The first hut exploded in fire, pursued by a second hut, then a third. Fire engulfed the compound. He watched the trucks leave with the women aboard. Jason returned to the relative safety of the tree house to inform Ford and arrange the next step.

Alvarez surveyed his destroyed farm as he climbed from the river. The only hut to escape the fire was Barba's old hut that he now shared with Blanca. Low in heart and filled with anger, he and Tomaz moved across the open space and entered the hut. Alvarez looked at the clock. It showed 12 noon.

Jason called Ford that all was ready, and he focused the laser spot on the hut roof. He saw the tiny image of the drone minutes later. A missile left it, heading towards its target. Tomaz looked out of the window as the missile hit the hut. Jason etched his face with the usual smirk. Jason looked at the scene of carnage, and he said into the phone to

Agent Ford, "La Fantasma exorcised. Balan, over and out."

CHAPTER 9

The trucks trundled along the dirt track with Cora seated on the passenger side, watching in the mirror for any sight of Alvarez or his men. On spotting the explosions, she knew Jason had completed his task, and she relaxed, but worried about him. She began looking around the cab, checking in door pockets and glove boxes. As she lowered the sun visor, she found a sat nav taped in place. She switched it on. It was useless to follow through the rainforest, but it recorded where a journey started and where it finished. It was important to get that information to Agent Ford as soon as possible.

Across the road lay a tree, making them come to a standstill.

Cora was relieved to discover Jason's crew put there it.

She knew the crew would have a satellite phone, and that she could now pass the information on regarding Barba's arranged rendezvous by the sea.

One of Jason's team gave instructions, which they all followed, and they soon arrived at the airstrip outside of Puerto Arango.

Ford had ordered the chopper to collect Jason, making his journey much quicker.

To see him safe and well, Cora was relieved. She rushed to greet him and planted a great big kiss on his lips.

"Cora," said Jason, "the play is over. We are back in normal life."

"I don't care," said Cora, giving him another kiss to the whoops and whistles from his team.

He gestured to give up. They followed him into a hut beside the strip. Seated around, they discussed what they knew. The shipment is going to Tumaco. The paperwork also identified the boat as number 237 and as being sold to them by North Korea for two and one-half million US dollars.

"We have to get there.

The standby pilot interrupted the conversation, saying, "I know we can get to the airport in Florencia in 10 minutes by chopper. Agent Ford has the tickets waiting for you. There is time to reach Tumaco."

Jason and Cora showered and changed into clothes their driver had relieved them of days before. Aboard the chopper, it whisked them off and landed at Florencia airport. Tickets were waiting at the desk for them, and they boarded the plane for Tumaco, once again playing the part of newlyweds.

They hailed a cab that took them to the center of town. They sat and examined the other truck's sat nav. The truck stopped beside the estuary behind the El sabrosito restaurant just south of the town.

"First, we need a car." Said Jason.

With wheels beneath them, they made their way along the San Jorge-Tumaco Road until they found the restaurant. A dirt track went off to the left as they drove past. They turned around and followed the track, progressing towards the estuary. No one else was there. They had arrived before the truck. They hid the car in shrubbery and waited.

There were lights coming down the dirt track in the morning. Jason and Cora watched as events unfolded. The men walked to the shoreline. They started flashing a torch, three shorts—one long—

three shorts—two longs; someone repeated the sequence over and over. An unseen person shone a repeating light, reversing the sequence, then nothing. They heard an outboard motor getting louder and louder. Jason and Cora watched a man disembark and shake hands with the two others. They moved to the rear of the truck and began unloading boxes and placing them in the inflatable. The man got back into the inflatable. The two from the truck lit cigarettes and waited. Thirty minutes later, the inflatable returned. They loaded more boxes on board before the boat left yet again. This occurred twice more, and the truck moved off. Cora and Jason started the car and raced back to the main road.

The truck had left. They turned towards the town and sped to watch the boat leave the estuary to join up with the outline of a submarine just before it sank beneath the waves.

Cora phoned and the information to agent Ford.

"OK," said Ford, "the Colombian navy frigate Almirante Padilla will trail the sub, and our navy will take over from them midway. Get yourselves back Stateside, guys, you have done a great job."

Jason and Cora returned to the airport and found tickets waiting for them to return to San Diego on the next flight with three connecting stops. Seated next to each other, both fall asleep.

"How was the flight?" asked Aaron Ford as he met them at San Diego airport.

"I wish you could have got us on a direct one," said Jason. "Three connections are not funny. Once sleep, we had to get ready to land, wait for ages for the next hop, wait again, hop, wait again. It was not the best flight I've been on."

"We wanted to get you here to watch events unfold," said Ford. "Our navy will shadow the sub as far as they can. So, rest up. The sub is running at 18 knots and will take about five days. Plenty of time for you to write up your reports. I booked you into a two-bed suite in the Marriott Marquis San

Diego Marina for you. Enjoy your stay. It is just yards from the marina, with magnificent views."

At the hotel, they booked in and shown to their suite. Jason threw himself on a bed and was asleep almost instantly. The bellhop woke him ten minutes later with a message.

"Sir, the madam wanted you to know she was going shopping." Without speaking, Jason slammed the door and returned to his bed.

"Shopping, who cares?" grumbled Jason as he drifted back off to sleep.

Jason woke to the sounds of screaming and crashing coming from the adjoining room. He could hear glass breaking and the men yelling threats. He opened the adjoining door to the sight of carnage. One man, shorter than the other, was trashing Cora's things. He went through bedside tables, hurling draws across the room. A balding man had straddled Cora, pinning down her arms with his knees, slapping her about, and demanding to know where Jason was.

He recalled what his father had taught him—only cowards hit girls and they will always fall. "Leave the girl alone, you coward," taunted Jason. "It's me you want."

The stocky, shorter one rushed towards Jason, head butting in his stomach, winding him, the other getting off Cora, swung a lamp at Jason's head, breaking the bulb, and cutting his temple. The shorter man returned to slapping Cora harder than before. He left Cora alone for a moment, and Shorty rushed at Jason. Jason side-stepped, spun, and slammed the man against the wall, knocking Baldy off his balance. Jason took advantage of it and thumped Baldy hard between the legs with a broken bed leg. Shorty rushed in again, Cora put her leg out and tripped him over; he fell against the broken glass from a picture frame. He collapsed there, gurgling and bleeding from where the glass now sat lodged in his jugular. The bellhop opened the door, seeing a fight, apologized and left, shutting the door. Undeterred, Jason punched and kicked out at Baldy. Baldy dropped to the floor and spun around whilst kicking out, catching Jason on the ankles hard enough to send him to the floor. Baldy struck out at him with a knife. Jason held his hands, stopping him. Cora darted to Baldy's back; he spun her around, smashing her against the wall and knocking her unconscious. Jason took his chance. He rose as Baldy came at him again with his knife. Jason parried it away and stabbed the open prongs of the lamp against Baldy's neck, who then fell backward. Jason drop-kicked his electrocuted adversary, assisting him in exiting through the broken balcony door and over the wall. On looking over the wall, Jason could see Baldy eight floors below, laying across a broken table beside the pool as hotel guests screamed. Jason was tending to an unconscious Cora as the hotel manager and security guards opened the door, followed by agent Ford.

Ford cleared a space on an unbroken chair beside what remained of a dressing table. He explained, "When they captured Cora, they took her photo and send it to a spy in Curillo Police. That man compared it with the photo taken of you two in the Bogota Museo-del-Oro. When the place blew up, he tried to reply, but failed. We had embedded an agent in Barba's gang some time ago. He was one of the two men you saw leaving the truck at Tumaco. It was him that told us. We found their spy when the chief of police forced everyone to hand over their phones, but not before he had informed on Cora to his boss in San Diego. They had her followed from the shopping mall to the hotel. That was how they came to rough up her up, seeking information on you."

"Poor Cora now has a price on her head because of him. I just hope he gets the rough justice he deserved," added Jason.

"He got that all right. He tried to escape and got shot by the police as he drew his gun," informed Ford. "It is a good thing they don't know Cora's real name; added to that, she's a Double B, and pink is not her normal lipstick color," said Ford.

"Double B? I'm sure that's not her bra size. She differs from that," replied Jason.

Ford laughed out loud, "BB is not her bra size. It means bottle blonde. Jason, you crease me up."

An embarrassed Jason asked after Cora's real name, but Ford refused to give it to him. "It's up to her to decide when to reveal it."

CHAPTER 10

The sub's captain spat a brown stream from his mouth as he chewed tobacco. He was rough, ready, and Russian. The cartel offered Captain Antipov a lot of money to run this side of their business after he retired from the Russian Navy. On his advice, they purchased the old soviet, 90-yard-long, rusting coffin from North Korea, which wanted American dollars quick. The Americans called this class of sub 'Juliette,' but it needed a Romeo or two to cheer it up. One could still see the outline of the old soviet red star; there were places where the painting failed. They painted the rest of the hulk dark gray before, but now it had more streaks of rust than paint.

Someone made quick repairs. They had applied fresh paint, making the side view look like a rejected Picasso picture.

The sub had 54 men on board in the Soviet days.

He would make do with far fewer, keeping costs down and his reward higher. He knew the sub could run at 18 knots below the waves. It would take 5 days each way.

With help from old colleagues, he altered the inside. There was no need for guided missile launching facilities. The 21-inch torpedoes interested him; he had a special use for them.

A constant drone from the diesel engines driving the twin propellers seemed to get louder by the minute. Reduced oxygen in the sub on the captain's orders would help prevent fires. The sweaty bodies of the sub and flatulence added to the rank air. The certainty of huge payouts kept the men going.

It was not possible to run on top. The captain feared being fired on by the frigate that was shadowing him. The pings from the sonar alerted him to its position. At periscope depth, he could see the Almirante Padilla following close behind.

All onboard were working a 12 on 12 off shift arrangement, with Captain Antipov passing control to Captain Lieutenant Kozar on rotation.

The third night into their journey, the screen showed two marks, with the sonar pings getting closer to each other. The two naval vessels were at the handover point. At periscope depth, Captain Antipov checked through his ship silhouette list of American cutters and recognized a legend class cutter, the USCGC Bertholf.

"I can't shake them off, but who cares? I have more tricks than one up my sleeve," said Antipov.

Two days later, they changed course, heading for the Gulf of California. They came to a standstill 100 miles to the west of Mazatlán. The USCGC Bertholf moved closer, monitoring proceedings. Antipov waited for dark before setting off going north, keeping to the central channel of the Gulf. The Bertholf followed two miles behind. Antipov slowed his sub, allowing the Bertholf to sit to the west of him. As they neared the west of Huatabampo near Navojoa. He ordered the torpedoes readied and the bow and aft doors to open. The Bertholf 'action stations' sounded. They had heard the torpedo doors opening and got ready for evasive action. The sub moved closer to the coastline. He watched for a small flashing light. Then fired four bow torpedoes in that direction and turned the sub and headed south. They picked the torpedoes being fired on the Bertholf and they sounded alarms. Within seconds, it became obvious they were not heading their way. The torpedoes were no longer running but had stopped. Bemused by events, the Captain on the Bertholf assumed the torpedoes had failed. He turned the cutter to follow the sub, much to the delight of Antipov.

The gulf of California was behind when Antipov headed for home. Captain Antipov led a Cossack dance, to the delight of the crew. Job done, money in the bank.

Two car recovery vehicles arrived at the beach and fixed a cable to the eyelet at the end of one torpedo; and towed it up the beach before fixing it on the truck. The second torpedo joined the first and covered with tarpaulins. Attention then switched to the other vehicle and the remaining torpedoes. The vehicles moved off down a dirt track, towards the main road that would take them to a safe garage in Hermosillo.

The team watched the garage after the tip-off. When the two car recovery vehicles enter the garage car park during the night, it triggered much interest. The place was dark when drivers left. Two agents climbed the fence and lifted the tarps to find the torpedoes.

Ford told them to stay and let him know when they leave.

Towards dawn, a truck arrived with Chilibonchas Watermelon Chilli Filled Hard Candy advertised on the sides.

The two agents watched as they broke customs seals and then opened the rear. They emptied most box's contents into two trash skips and refilled the boxes with the contents of the torpedoes before closing up the doors.

The third man arrived in a uniform. He resealed the truck and left after getting an envelope.

The agents were taking photos with their mobile phones all the time and sending them to Agent Ford.

The agents followed the truck at a distance so they wouldn't raise suspicion. Two and one-half hours later, the truck passed beside the Servicio

Matelo. An old Mexican man phoned Ford, "the trucks heading to Nogales."

"I bet he plans to go through the Border post there," said Aaron Ford.

The truck waited in line at the border until called forward. Agent Ford sat beside a monitor, watching the proceedings. They scanned the underside, and they checked the custom seal along with the paperwork. The dog handler moved around the outside of the truck without reaction. Ford said to break the seal and have the dog check the inside. It moved around, sniffing everywhere, and leaped down from the truck, finding nothing. "Open a box," instructed Ford. "Show it to the dog." The dog was not interested. "Hide a transmitter and let it go," he said.

"Put a tail on him," said Ford.

Turn taking, the agents followed the truck for the next eight hours until it arrived on the outskirts of San Diego. The agents following kept the truck in their sights whilst playing leapfrog; it turned into a side road to a workshop behind closed doors.

The DEA agents began surveillance duty, observing all that entered the workshop. A black Mercedes pulled up. A man got out. "Clarkson. He's the cartel's new leader since the death of Alvarez," said Ford. "Who's that bandaged man behind him?" Asked Ford, continuing the discussion. "He looks like the invisible man or a bandaged Egyptian mummy." Ford quipped.

Armed DEA agents surrounded the workshop dressed in bullet-proof vests. On Ford's command, they smashed the door in with a heavy Ford truck, and the agents flooded in, ordering all to raise their hands, declaring they were DEA agents. In desperation, some fired shots at the agents who returned deadly fire. Clarkson raised his hands, resigned to his fate. They led the gang off in handcuffs. The bandaged man had disappeared.

Ford sat at a desk in the DEA office and invited Jason to enter.

"Jason, a fantastic job, well done. Clarkson has evaded us for years; he was a top man in the cartel and slippery as a greased pig. We have him booked. He will serve long and hard. I handed the packets with the cocaine to our laboratory to find out how they evaded detection. Have no fear, we will stop their game from now on. It might also interest you the Colombian National Police, along with their Navy, sank the sub before it entered its hideout in the islands around Amarales. The boat went down with all hands."

There was a knock on the door. Jason could not see who it was. Ford said, "Come in and join us."

Jason turned to see a stunning brunette dressed in a knee-length floral dress. She smiled at him.

"I know her from somewhere," mussed Jason.

The brunette spoke and Jason a recognized Cora. "Wow..." stuttered Jason.

"You two deserve a holiday. Two weeks expenses paid for in the Best where you stayed before, Sorry Cora, but your room is still out of action for a time, it needs refurbishing," said Agent Ford, "before I forget, did you get anywhere with that cyber note?"

"No. I assume it has been a problem for cryptologists in the office as well."

The two walked towards the hotel. Cora turned toward Jason and said, "My real name is Claire Wright. How do you do?"

As she slipped her hand into his, she said, "I might have nightmares about fish."

"Don't worry," said Jason. "I know someone who would come to your aid."

"Mmm," said Claire.

"The jaguar has his quarry, now for the meal…" chuckled Jason.

CHAPTER 11

Jason Balan stood beside the grimy window in his air-conditioned office, watching the traffic on the road below. Someone knocked on the office door. His boss, Aaron Ford, entered, not waiting for an answer.

"I wanted to see you before you leave. I just wanted to let you know that they never found Alvarez's body. That ghost had disappeared yet again." "Was any progress made on that cipher?" Asked Ford.

"Claire had some thoughts." Replied Jason.

"She thinks a double cipher. Look, I'm just going past her office; I'll get her to come up to you in a minute." Said Ford.

He left a lot of words and numbers on the piece of paper.

Jason was reading the accompanying report when Claire popped her head around the door.

"Hi Jason, have you looked at the note? Oh, before I forget, did you pay the deposit for the Miami apartment?" Asked Claire.

"Deposit yes, note no. I'm interested in the report, though," replied Jason. "They never found Alvarez's body. He disappeared again. That man is a ghost."

He and Claire read the report, informing them that the latest piece of paper was inside a secret compartment in the right shoe heel of a black African Caribbean. His photograph ties up with that of a suspected drug courier based in Barbados. There was a receipt from the Marriot Hotel, paid for on a stolen Visa credit card in the name of Rufus Delaney. On the third of July, they discovered his body behind bushes in the verdant Bayfront Park off Biscayne Boulevard. Shot twice through the head. His assassin used a silencer. With the body was an incendiary device hidden inside a briefcase that had failed to ignite had it done so; we would have nothing at all. "The hotel is a mile and a half away from Bayfront Park; that is where we should begin questioning." Said Jason.

"I agree," replied Claire. "Let us explore our options when we get to the apartment. Am I cooking tonight?"

"Neh, don't cook, we can stop and get something Mexican." Responded Jason.

"Sounds good to me," replied Claire as she gathered the photocopies and placed the original piece of paper back into a small fire-safe behind Jason's desk.

They left the office together and walked to the car park where Jason had left his machine gray roadster. He could afford a more upmarket ride, but he just loved the agility of the Mazda. They stopped and collected the Mexican food Jason had ordered before and headed back to their apartment.

They finished their meal and changed into loose, casual clothes. Claire curled up on the sofa with a pencil-and-paper pad whilst Jason sprawled out on the carpet, scratching away on a piece of paper with a gel pen. Claire laughed at him and asked, "Why don't you use a pencil? You will get less on your face."

Jason wiped his face with the back of his hand, only making matters worse. He looked in the mirror above the fireplace. Jason saw why Claire was laughing. He had camouflaged his face in blue ink.

"I'm just going to the bathroom to use your war paint remover," he quipped.

He accepted a pencil offered to him by a smirking Claire and returned to the matter at hand.

"I don't get this. Who would write this way?" asked Jason. He continued, "prompt guarding earl? This can't be an English speaker. It's not even a correct sentence. I reckon it could be a code."

"It is not a code, it may be a cipher," said Claire. "I have played with the words assuming it to be a ciphertext-alphabet in reverse with letters meaning digits, but they did not group them as expected. The text is not a Vigenère cipher."

Jason yawned and said, "I guess so. This lot has made my head hurt. I'm ready for bed. Let's get an early start tomorrow and visit the Marriott. You never know what we might find."

Sleep came, and even Jason's jagged snoring didn't disturb Claire.

After showering and quick continental breakfasts. The pair dressed and drove to the Marriott Hotel. They parked up and entered the large hotel lobby with its high ceilings and unique art on display. The pair walked to a free receptionist, identified themselves, and asked for the manager.

The manager greeted them in a side office and introduced himself as Mr. Spencer Nelson.

He explained the police requested no housekeeping in the room. "I have handed the police a computer printout about Mr. Delaney; I have your copy here," he said and passed over a single page of printed text.

Mr. Nelson continued, "Mr. Delaney booked in and paid in advance for two days. He ordered nothing, nor did he ring reception. CCTV shows his arrival on his own and that he left on his own. May I escort you to his guestroom?"

The room overlooked the bay. Mr. Delaney had left no clothing. The bed appeared unused, aside from being a little disheveled. Someone moved the chair by the fixed desk/table, fingerprint powder was on its back and on the table where forensic officers had dusted, leaving an outline of a pen or pencil in the dust.

Jason pointed to the ruffled bedding, moved to the cabinet, and opened the drawer. Inside were two books, a Gideon Bible, and a Book of Mormon, which he lifted out and flipped through the pages before replacing them.

"Hmm," voiced Jason, "you always get the same in every Marriott Hotel, did you know the founder of the Marriott hotel chain was a member of the Church of Jesus Christ of Latter-Day Saints, better known by their nickname—Mormons? His son now runs the business and is very active in the church."

"I think we're through here," said Claire. "Let's return to the office. Someone may have cracked those three words."

"Three words? What three words? Do you mean the cipher?" Said Jason.

Claire produced a screech and said, "that's it, repeat what you just said."

"I only said what three words?" Replied a puzzled Jason.

"Search for the what3words app for your phone and run it. Enter the set that we worked on last night, prompt guarding earl, and put a full stop between each word with no spacing," insisted Claire. "Come on, Jason, what does it say?"

"No wonder you are an intelligence officer. It has identified this hotel entrance. We can check on the other word groups in the office. I'm sure that what you discovered will intrigue Aaron Ford," uttered Jason.

Aaron Ford sat back in his chair as Jason and Claire entered his office. "Well?" he asked. "anything for me?"

Ford listened as Jason and Claire explained how their quarry used the app to find specific places for unknown reasons. They reasoned the numbers were for time and date.

"As we visit the other locations, we will keep working on the digit strings. It is a mystery why they have used Marriott hotels multiple times.

"Jason, Tyrone Griffith is Commissioner of the Royal Barbados Police Force (RBPF) and I have just spoken with him, and he has given permission for you to carry a gun but advised of firearms restriction use when necessary to confront an imminent threat of death or serious injury or a grave and proximate threat to life," instructed Ford.

Jason moved his left arm against his Federal Shoulder Holster beneath his jacket, but Ford observed his action.

He continued with emphasis, "I must repeat his instruction, do not draw your Glock unless there is an imminent threat to life. Do you understand?"

"Message received and understood," replied Jason.

Ford continued, "I booked you on the American Airways flight tonight at 20.00 hours, arriving about twenty to midnight. When you arrive at Grantley Adams International Airport, Mr. Keith Sergeant will meet you; as the Chief Customs officer, he knows you are on that flight. He will escort you through immigration and customs," explained Ford. "A shuttle service will take you to the Marriott hotel in Bridgetown. A car is at your disposal in the morning. They drive on the wrong side of the road.

don't have any accidents. This is 't an island-

hopping holiday."

CHAPTER 12

The flight to Grantley Adams Airport was uneventful except for a Rastafarian playing Nyabinghi music with its chanting and drumming loud on his ghetto blaster.

He rejected the pleadings of mothers with screaming children, and he ignored Flight assistants and their warnings.

Jason could stand it no longer. He rose from his seat and crossed the aisle. He leaned down and whispered in the man's ear. "If you don't want to wake up later with a pain in your jaw, turn your music off."

The Rastafarian shrugged his shoulders as he opened his eyes. He was ready with a quick quip until he saw Jason's six-foot-three muscular frame standing over him. Thinking it wiser to comply, he turned the ghetto blaster off but continued to tap out its rhythm on the seat in front. Jason placed his enormous hand over the man's and pressed down. Jason enforced his desire with a firm squeeze on the man's hand, which encouraged a brief yelp to emanate from the man's mouth.

"Sit still and quiet," said Jason as he returned to his seat. He smiled and nodded at another man in an aisle seat.

Claire enquired after Jason's acquaintance.

"The man at the back?" Responded Jason. "He is an air marshal. I saw him get on board. He is aware of our presence on the flight."

The other passengers expressed their thanks with a round of clapping and shouts of thanks to Jason's embarrassment as the Rastafarian pressed his body lower into his seat as if trying to hide.

The plane touched down, and officers directed passengers toward immigration.

A well-dressed man stood beneath a 'Welcome to Barbados' sign. He spotted Jason and Claire and approached them.

"Good evening," he said, "I am Keith Sergeant. I assume Aaron Ford sent here you."

"Hi, yes," said Jason. "I am Jason Balan, and this is—"

"Claire Wright," interrupted Claire as she extended her hand.

Keith Sergeant escorted them through immigration, aside from the noise of frustrated passengers opening suitcases.

"They don't like us doing these spot checks. So much contraband enters it is something we have to do," explained Keith Sergeant.

Above the passengers, Nyabinghi music was being blasted.

"Him again," offered Jason.

"He was playing it on the plane until Jason asked him to stop," said Claire.

Keith Sergeant laughed at her comment with a knowing grin.

Jason and Claire climbed aboard the old yellow Zed R shuttle bus ahead of all the other passengers and sat down together. The bus filled, and the hubbub began again. Above the noise of the passengers, Nyabinghi music was being blasted. Passengers begged the man to stop. Jason stood up, and the bus went quiet. The player of the music turned around. Jason was standing behind a large lady with a yellow head wrap. Jason never spoke, just glared. The man turned the music off and pressed himself into the metal-framed seat. With peace restored, the cackle of voices in the overloaded bus began again as Jason sat down.

The drive of the Zed R shuttle bus took the scenic route to the hotel, dropping people off

"I'll be happy to get to the hotel and bed.," Claire said.

"Mmmm," responded Jason.

Distant lights became brighter, and soon the Zed R stopped outside the Marriott Courtyard Hotel.

People were milling around the lobby. Jason and Claire made their way to the desk, where two young ladies sat behind enormous computer screens. They booked them in with big, welcoming smiles. Aaron Ford had made reservations for an extensive suite for them facing the sea.

A pleasant young bellman arrived and placed their luggage on a trolley and led the way to the elevator.

"Are you here on business or pleasure?" asked the bellman.

"Both," responded Claire.

"I hear you had a little excitement a few days ago," said Jason, seeking information.

"Oh yes," came the response. "Two days ago, a man got stabbed with a large knife. Strange that he wasn't staying here. The police were everywhere. We were told not to discuss it. It just meant more work for us."

Jason looked at Claire and nodded.

The bellman pushed the trolley along the carpeted hallway to open the door. He then gave a mini tour around the suite. Jason thanked him and pressed an American bill into his hand as the bellman left.

Jason began disrobing. Claire dropped her outer garments as she made her way towards the shower before him. When she returned, Jason had fallen asleep on the bed. Claire pulled a cover over him, crawled beneath the sheets beside him, and was soon asleep.

As morning broke, Claire slipped out of bed and entered the ensuite and stepped inside the shower. Jason was still asleep when she returned to their bedroom. She sat the desk and opened the envelope left for them by Commissioner Tyrone Griffith.

She sat reading, unaware that Jason had risen and had moved across the plush carpet and stood behind her whilst reading over her shoulder. Claire jumped when Jason broke the silence with a cough.

They read the report together: the victim was a black male, around 30 years of age, and appeared to be a Bajan and follower of the Rastafarian religion.

They had circulated his photo around the island, and the commissioner expected his identification soon. A single stab wound with a long-bladed knife had entered his back on the left of center and thrust deep into his heart, killing him. Death would have been instant. From his position on the bed, he appeared to have been asleep on his front when the attack occurred. The report noted that he had not registered at the hotel. The reason he was there was unknown. They eliminated the previous residents. They had taken a boat cruise to Saint Vincent, returning after they had found the body. The report included photos of the crime scene and the victim's personal property.

Jason examined the photos with care. The corpse was laying face down. A Book of Mormon was hanging out of the bedside cabinet.

"More notes?" asked Jason.

As Claire flipped through the paperwork, she found another slip of paper. It was another group of words and strings of digits, as before.

"We are one up on them. Type into the What3words app on your phone the following," said Claire, "unsteady addictions months. Where does it take us?"

"We're in the island's north. It is at a place called Animal Flower Cave." Replied Jason. "Let's get over there now."

"Wait," said Claire. "Let's look in the guidebook that may help us first."

It didn't take long for Claire to read that Animal Flower Cave was a sea cave and was accessible down a steep flight of wet steps.

Claire noted, permitted swimming in the cave. "I think it would be prudent to take swimming gear with us," she suggested.

Directed by the lady at the desk in the lobby, they soon found the car Aaron Ford had arranged for them in the hotel car park.

"Remember to drive on the wrong side of the road," teased Claire.

Claire had dressed to keep cool in a flowing sarong tied on her left hip, exposing part of her slender left leg as she walked in sturdy flip-flops. Jason and Claire had been a couple since their time in Columbia, but that did not stop him from admiring Claire's beauty.

With her seated to his left in the passenger seat, her left leg appeared during the journey, eliciting instructions from Claire to keep his eyes and mind on the road.

It was an hour's drive from the hotel in Bridgetown to the Saint Lucy district, going past sugar cane plantations and local wildlife of goats and sheep before following white-painted signs pointing to the cave carpark.

CHAPTER 13

An old, dirty white saloon car screeched out of hiding and headed towards them, as Jason and Claire walked across the car park. He dived to his left and pushed Claire the other way. The car spun around as Jason drew his Glock. He put four shots into the saloon. One of them hit the driver on the shoulder, causing the car to make a jerky movement, giving Claire and Jason time to find shelter beside the souvenir shop. Jason took aim and put a slug in the driver's chest. The pair watched as the saloon sped up and crashed through the barrier and nose-dived over the cliff towards a wet grave.

He said it should help wash away his sins.

"They knew we were here." said Claire

"Ratted on or followed." Suggested Jason.

"No fireball occurred on the crash," said Claire.

The two rushed to the car. Claire slipped on the wet steps in her excitement, but Jason caught her pulling her to safety.

"This is getting to be a habit. Me saving you from something bad." quipped Jason through a smile. "First it was a little fish. Then a frog looked at you after a snake slithered between your legs. Again at Barba's camp, and at the hotel in a fight. Now you can't seem to hold on to the safety rope. I think I have to be with you more for your safety."

Claire smiled back and gave Jason a loving punch on the arm.

The Animal Flower Cave was to the left of the wrecked car. They examined the inside of the car wreckage. The crash pressed the dead man against the steering wheel. When he fished through his pockets, he discovered two folded pieces of paper and an envelope. Three items were now in his pocket. Jason moved away from the car. Shots rang out. Two men were running down the steps. Jason returned fire. He and Claire ran for cover in the cave. Jason ushered Claire to the far end and together they slipped into the water and waited. The inside was dark against the cave opening. It silhouetted everyone against the sky.

The two gunmen stood in the cave entrance, and just as Jason supposed, they could not hide themselves. They blindly fired into the cave whilst Jason picked his target with care and fired a single round, hitting the first man. He fired at the second man before he could go to cover, hitting him with a single shot. Both had dropped into the water, coloring it red with blood. Jason and Claire waited a while in case of others seeking their death.

They returned to the car park dripping wet from their unscheduled swim in the cave. "What did you find in his pocket?" asked Claire when they sat in the car.

"Two more messages and a small envelope." Jason said.

"You drive," said Claire, "and I check them out."

Claire ripped open the envelope and found another coded message.

"I think we may have a new message before they acted upon it," said Claire

She checked with what3words. "First, the hotel we are staying at. Second the cave. The one in the envelope reads 'extent speaks debit' points to

Skeete's Bay on the east of the island, and there is a jetty there. I'm inclined to think it is worth a look. "

"Yes, I believe it is," said Jason as he typed Skeete's Bay into the sat nav and they began their journey.

Their route took them over mountain roads under various conditions. Some little more than dirt tracks. A car swung out from a hidden road behind scrubland, shattering the beauty of the vista. The car sped up and shunted Jason and Claire. Jason sped up, but the other driver matched his speed. Another rear-end shunt followed, then an attempt to PIT maneuver but Jason, now aware of the other's intention, accelerated. He then turned his car in a handbrake turn to face the other driver. Then drove towards the other car, avoiding the edge of the mountain road. The other had to move. Jason steered into the car and pushed him over the road's edge.

He turned their car around to continue their journey. Moments later, another car joined the deadly chase. This time, as the following car got close, the passenger opened fire, putting a shot between Jason and Claire through the back window and out via the windscreen. Jason passed his Glock to Claire and told her to aim for the tires. It took a few shots to hit the tire of the next car. Sparks showered from the wheel rim. He seized the opportunity, moved close to the safe edge of the road, slowed, and forced the other car to pass him. He pushed the other car over the edge.

They pulled up to watch as the second car traveled down the scrub-covered mountainside before bursting into flames as it collided with a tree.

"Nothing left down there." Jason quipped.

Claire. said, "we might as well continue to Skeete's Bay and see what it offers."

Their drive through Barbados countryside continued until they turned left at the signpost fixed to a telegraph pole, pointing towards Skeete's Bay. Jason and Claire drove past various building sites along a worn-out tarmac road down a hill. The road finished at a large yellow painted building. To the right, palm trees went down to the sea before meeting rocky outcrops. A few fishing boats were bobbing on the sea, along with others pulled up on to the beach near the palm trees. They knew this was an important site. It was in the envelope. They assumed they would arrive at a location before the drug dealers. Ahead was the wooden jetty, with a patchwork of flooring slabs. Jason looked around and noticed large swathes of orange seaweed drying on the beach where tides had thrown it. The faint echoes of music added to the sounds of the beach. A man was sitting on the jetty. He rested against a street lamp. He was playing music on a blaster whilst he looked out at the sea as he played the music with his fingers.

Jason and Claire walked along the jetty. The music became clear and louder. "Not again," hissed Jason. The Nyabinghi rhythmic drumming music and chanting were loud enough to silence the sound of crashing waves and the sound of their footsteps.

Shadows alerted the man to their presence as they came right beside him.

"Hello again," said Jason. "Still playing your music too loud."

The Rastafarian jumped up, knocking his music system into the water, making him angry. He pulled a gun from under his shirt. Before he had time to take aim, Jason shot him. He fell backwards into the sea. The waves were slow to take him and calm return.

Claire and Jason sat down where the Rastafarian had sat and contacted Commissioner Tyrone Griffith and Agent Ford. Both had to be informed of Jason's actions to protect their lives. Griffith said he would get the various scenes cleaned before wishing them to keep safe.

The pair watched as a distant ship lowered something into the sea. Keeping themselves hidden by the metal structure at the end of the jetty. The ship remained stationary.

There were no fishing boats near the anchored boat, causing Claire and Jason to suppose it had nothing nefarious in its actions, and passed nothing to a small boat to bring it ashore. They thought it would be a good idea to sit and wait.

They kept watch and snuggled against each other. The peace shattered when a black minisub surfaced at the end of the jetty. The pilot spoke in English as the cockpit slid back. "Rashied, are you there?"

"He got held up. I'm here for him." shouted Jason as he removed his shirt and holster in a hurry whilst kicking off his shoes. As he part showed himself, Claire rolled his trouser legs up, removed his socks, and held on to his Glock.

"Show yourself." came the response.

"Sure," said Jason as he moved into the open.

"What happened to Rashied, and what's your name?" questioned the man.

Jason thought and shouted back his grandfather's name, "Huracan Balan."

The pilot asked where he came from.

"I was Alvarez's man in the Yucatan. They sent me over here to help."

Satisfied with the responses, the pilot shouted out to Jason to catch. He threw a heavy bag over to him. "See you next week."

The minisub hatch closed, and it disappeared below the waves, turning back the way it came. Jason and Claire watched it being hoisted back on the boat, and the original boat sailed off into the distance.

With the boat out of sight, they contacted agent Ford. They had interrupted the drug route into Barbados.

CHAPTER 14

Jason rested against the lamp post looking back along the jetty when his thoughts cut short by a knocking sound. They found nothing on the jetty.

In the sea, they saw the Rastafarian's ghetto blaster bobbing in the water, knocking against the wood posts.

Jason dropped his pants and lowered into the water to recover the item. He swung it back on the jetty, landing near where Claire stood.

"His music is all washed away now," said Jason, pulling himself up.

"Something made him angry when it fell into the sea?"

The battery compartment was loose and Jason opened it. Inside were several small envelopes, each numbered from one to six. Together with a list of contacts, locations, times and dates.

She said, "The drugs destinations we have, likewise the time and dates. The Rastafarian was the cartel's mailman for the island. He was noisy, visible and hidden in full view."

Back at the hotel, Jason and Claire examined the gym bag's contents. There were 10 one kilo bags of pills in sealed plastic wrapping. They appeared to look like the bags of coke wrapped and shipped from Barba's place in Colombia. Along with the coke, there was a larger envelope containing five credit cards in different names, and a Book of Mormon.

Jason spoke whilst passing the book to Claire, "I know many Mormons, but not one that would be a drug mule or dealer. Why put it in the gym bag?"

As she flipped through the pages, Claire said, "that is an excellent question. Maybe they're using it for an Ottendorf cipher. Every hotel room contains the book. All are identical. It would make sense. They can check the messages in the hotel without carrying the book around. Both correspondents need the same text. All the books seen are identical, and I reason the book is the key."

Jason suggested they hold a conference call with Agent Ford and Commissioner Tyrone to inform them of the discoveries.

With all four parties connected, Jason explained their discoveries. He suggested they will use the minisub method as they did today to bring a ready supply onto the island.

They knew the dealers' names and location.

He recommended a co-ordinated early hours swoop across Barbados, but do it after the mother boat and minisub capture.

With the documents they had seized, Claire will feed the information back.

They agreed to the plan. Jason would wait on the jetty at Skeete's Bay, at 12 o'clock as before. The sub pilot would recognize him. Wait until the drugs are on the jetty and the minisub leaves. The custom boats will then come out of hiding behind Bell Point to capture the mother boat as they lift the sub.

Agent Ford instructed Jason's team to fly to Barbados, leaving from California and Florida.

They arrived in small groups not to alert anyone and booked into various hotels around the island.

They gathered together in a conference suite at the Marriotts hotel to receive instructions. The commissioner knew that some of his police force were dirty. He selected those he could trust to be the links between the DEA and the force. A technician flew in from Miami to conduct a bug sweep of the conference suite. They didn't want the information being leaked outside. Normal Marriott employees had their duties changed to ensure no one would know how important the meeting was.

The doors locked on the inside and they gave assignments out. Small teams would visit the suspects' homes. It was imperative that they were all rounded up before they could alert anyone else.

Surveillance of suspects' homes took the rest of the week up. Claire continued her work with the cipher.

Agent Aaron Ford coordinated all information, working alongside Commissioner Tyrone Griffith, with Jason attending all their meetings.

Before 12 noon on the identical day of the week, Jason sat shirtless and shoeless beside the last lamp post on Skeete's Bay jetty. He rolled his trouser legs up halfway between knee and ankle. Jason hid his Glock under his shirt with his shoes on top. Out to sea, he watched the mother ship, lowering in the sub. At 12 o'clock, the minisub surfaced, and the pilot called out, "Rashied, are you there?"

Jason called back and said, "No, it's me, Huracan Balan. Rashied can't make it again."

Jason moved to be seen by the minisub pilot. "Hi Huracan, good to see you. How are you?" Asked the pilot.

"Well enough," said Jason. He continued, "be better when I pass on our product to our distributers, though."

The pilot laughed out, "yeah, catch." He threw the gym bag to Jason, who opened it to check its contents.

"Take care and I'll catch you later," said a smiling Jason, who waved the other good bye.

Drug Enforcement Administration agents were watching the events on the jetty and waiting for the drugs to arrive. They focused all eyes on the boat.

The minisub surfaced to the rear of the mother boat that raised it. On cue, the Barbados custom boats came out from Bell Point and tore across the water at high speed. The minisub dropped to the water.

Custom boats surrounded the ship. Officers climbed aboard and a small gun fight ensued. Without warning, the minisub surfaced, and the pilot climbed out. His anger boiling over, he kept referring to the custom agents as illegitimate sons of whores.

The pilot asked for help. He continued, "Alvarez is on the boat and it is booby-trapped to explode if stopped by customs or the DEA."

"OK, how is my old boss, Alvarez?" Asked Jason.

"He is fuming about two DEA agents called Jason and Cora. They blew up his farm in Columbia, killing many of his men. He only escaped by chance. When a missile hit the hut, he had bent down into Barba's heavy fridge. Alvarez survived but burned. He put a bounty of one million dollars on the agents. He was sending their photos from the ship using a plug-and-play device which can connect to the internet 20 miles from the shore. I would have got mine after I dropped your gear off. I put their photos in the bag for you. Let me show you."

Before Jason could stop him, the pilot had opened the bag and pulled out the photos and realized one was of Jason, who dropped to the jetty floor and recovered his Glock from under his shirt.

"You have a choice to make," said Jason, "you will either die here, spend a lifetime in prison, or become an informer and turn states evidence. Your choice."

As Jason finished speaking, a tremendous explosion onboard the boat sent flames hundreds of feet into the air. There was no chance of survival.

Less than a minute later, the boat sank without survivors. Those custom officers still in their boats searched the waters for anyone still alive. They found none, all were dead. Other boats arrived to help collect bodies.

"Have you made your decision yet?" Asked Jason.

He realized he had no way out. He agreed to become a witness for the state, giving up all the names he knew.

A car arrived for Jason and the pilot. They took him to the central police station in Bridgetown. On the journey, Jason discovered the man's name was Talin Boyce, who lived in Fitts Village on the west coast with his wife Marissa, his year old daughter, Lesia.

Jason had to request more paper to write on from the driver. Boyce had much to tell. On arrival, they took Boyce into custody and processed him. Agent Ford arrived with the commissioner.

"Fantastic job Jason." Said Ford. "Guess whose body they found floating on the sea, Alvarez's. Now he is a ghost."

Commissioner Tyron thanked Jason but expressed deep sorrow for the custom officers killed in the line of duty. "You may like to know. We hit everyone on the list. The whole drug ring is gone. I have also recommended you for special commendation. You'll hear about it in the future.

Thank you on behalf of all Bajans."

CHAPTER 15

Jason and Claire settled down in their rented car, taking in sights, smells, and sounds of their Caribbean trip as they made their lazy way back to the airport and flight back to Florida. Job completed.

"I am so impressed with you working out how they passed messages around. You are a great intelligence specialist, Claire."

She chuckled out an answer with a giggle. "It couldn't be too difficult seeing some of those that used it. I have the last message we found to decipher."

Claire opened the Book of Mormon she had borrowed from the hotel, and began flipping through the pages, only stopping to write a word.

Jason checked his watch. It was just before twelve. On the other side of the road, taking up all available space, was an elderly ice cream seller peddling his wares. After driving past the layby, Jason pulled the car onto the grass verge and turned the engine off. Claire noted Jason seemed a little preoccupied. He seemed nervous.

"I would love an ice cream with a good sprinkle of pistachios on top," she asked, whilst fluttering eyelids at him, all thrown in for good measure.

Jason moved around the car and opened Claire's door.

"What are you doing?" she enquired. "Are we getting out?"

Without answering, Jason put his hand in his pocket, pulled out a small box, and dropped to one knee. Claire and Jason had been an item for sometime, ever since spending weeks in the Jungle on their first assignment together. His actions now caught her by total surprise, but set her heart all a quiver waiting for an assumed question.

"Claire, I know something destined us for each other," Jason sounded choked up, but stammered out, "Claire Wright, will you marry? Please?" He implored.

"Jason, you have made today the happiest day of my life. Yes, of course I will marry you." She responded, adding, "In a heartbeat, if you get extra pistachios on my ice cream."

"Anything you want," answered Jason as he slipped a diamond ring on her left ring finger.

He leaned inside the car and gave her a long, hard, lingering kiss, then making his way across the road and towards the ice cream seller. Claire looked long and hard at her engagement ring. With a big smile on her face, she turned her attention to the message.

Jason approached the ice cream seller and ordered Claire's pistachio's coated cornet and requested a regular ice cream with strawberry sauce for himself.

Without warning, an enormous explosion from behind him threw him against the seller's truck. Instinctively, his hand went for his Glock. His car crashed back to the ground as he turned around. All past thoughts about Claire raced through his mind. He knew his soulmate was dead. He wanted to be beside her. Life now appeared meaningless to him.

He knew there was nothing he could do for his love. He hated those who had deprived him of a happy life with Claire. The perpetrators wanted to kill them. They destroyed Claire, but he survived.

Through tears, he watched charred pieces of paper drift down. One landed close to his feet. He stooped and picked it up. Claire was working on a cipher as he left her in the car. She must have finished it before the bomb exploded.

Jason looked hard at the paper. It read: "298.6.12 - 341.35.10 - 2.9.30" beneath the digits Claire had deciphered them as "destroy-both-noon." They had targeted him and Claire for death.

She added a footnote that read: Book of Mormon, page number, verse number, word number.

As a little tease for Jason, Claire added a new set of digits for him to decipher: 463.40.46 and 123.8.21

Jason sat down on the roadside, dropped his head, and sobbed.

THE END

Printed in Great Britain
by Amazon

36436997R00121